A Book of Rhymes by

Rodney Peppé

Holt, Rinehart and Winston
New York   Chicago   San Francisco

MOUSE

For Stephen Drawbell

Other books by Rodney Peppé

THE ALPHABET BOOK
CIRCUS NUMBERS
THE HOUSE THAT JACK BUILT
HEY RIDDLE DIDDLE!
SIMPLE SIMON

A Holt Reinforced Edition

Copyright © 1973 by Rodney Peppé
ISBN : 0-03-010321-5

Library of Congress Catalog Card Number : 73-1569

Originally published in England by Longman Young Books Ltd.
Printed in Belgium by Offset Printing Van Den Bossche ☒
First American Edition

Jack Sprat
Had a cat,
It had but one ear;
It went to buy butter
when butter was dear.

Three blind mice, see how they run!
They all ran after the farmer's wife,

Who cut off their tails with a carving knife,
Did you ever see such a thing in your life,
As three blind mice?

Pussy cat Mole jumped over a coal
And in her best petticoat burnt a great hole.
Poor pussy's weeping, she'll have no more milk
Until her best petticoat's mended with silk.

I saw a ship a-sailing,
　A-sailing on the sea;
And Oh! it was laden
　With pretty things for thee.

There were comfits in the cabin,
　And apples in the hold,
The sails were made of silk,
　And the masts of beaten gold.

The four and twenty sailors
　That stood between the decks
Were four and twenty white mice
　With chains about their necks.

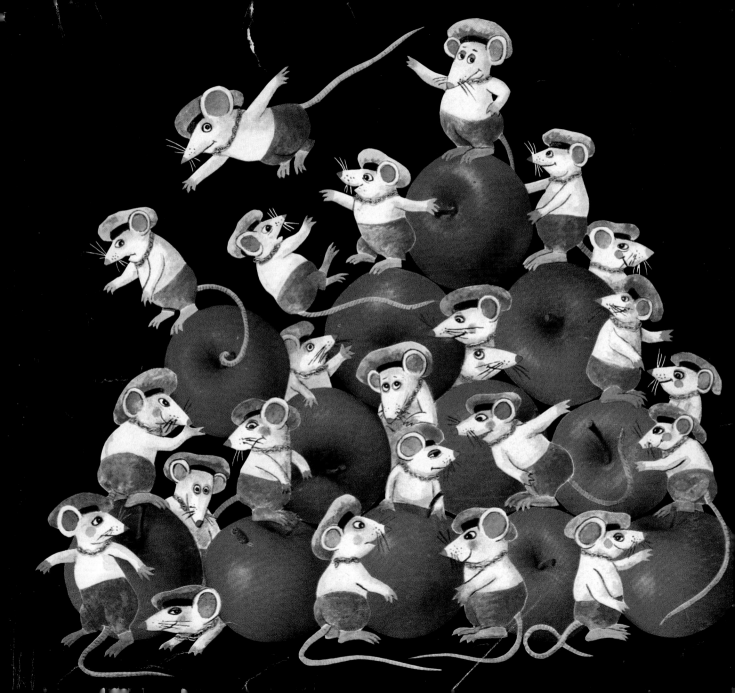

The Captain was a duck,
  With a packet on his back,
And when the ship began to move
  The Captain said Quack! Quack!

Jack Hall,
He is so small.
A mouse could eat him,
Hat and all.

Little Poll Parrot
  Sat in a garret
Eating toast and tea;
  A little brown mouse,
  Jumped into the house,
And stole it all away.

Pussy cat, pussy cat,
Where have you been?
I've been to London
To look at the Queen.

Pussy cat, pussy cat,
  What did you there?
I frightened a little mouse
  under a chair.

Diddlety, diddlety, dumpty,
The cat ran up the plum tree;
  Half a crown
  To fetch her down,
Diddlety, diddlety, dumpty.

Ride away, ride away,
 Johnny shall ride,
He shall have a pussy cat
 Tied to one side;
He shall have a little dog
 Tied to the other,
And Johnny shall ride
 To see his grandmother.

There was an old woman
Lived under a hill,
She put a mouse in a bag,
And sent it to the mill.

The miller did swear
   By the point of his knife
He never took toll
   Of a mouse in his life.

There was a crooked man
And he walked a crooked mile;
He found a crooked sixpence
Against a crooked stile;

He bought a crooked cat,
Which caught a crooked mouse,
And they all lived together
In a little crooked house.

Six little mice sat down to spin;
Pussy passed by and she peeped in.
What are you doing, my little men?
Weaving coats for gentlemen.

Shall I come in and cut off your threads?
No, no, Mistress Pussy, you'd bite off our heads.
Oh, no, I'll not; I'll help you to spin.
That may be so, but you don't come in.

Hickory, dickory, dock,
The mouse ran up the clock.

The clock struck one,
The mouse ran down,
Hickory, dickory, dock.

Dame Trot and her cat
Sat down for a chat;
The dame sat on this side
And the puss sat on that.

Puss says the dame,
   Can you catch a rat,
Or a mouse in the dark?
   Purr, says the cat.

Round about, round about,
Catch a wee mouse;
Up a bit, up a bit,
In a wee house.

Little Tom Tittlemouse
Lived in a bell-house;
The bell-house broke,
And Tom Tittlemouse woke.

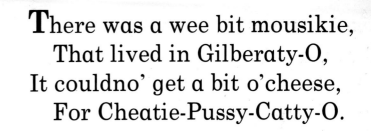

There was a wee bit mousikie,
That lived in Gilberaty-O,
It couldno' get a bit o'cheese,
For Cheatie-Pussy-Catty-O.

It said unto the cheesiky,
"Oh fain, would I be at ye-O
If'twere no' for the cruel claws
O' Cheatie-Pussy-Catty-O."

Ding, dong, bell,
Pussy's in the well.
Who put her in?
Little Johnny Green.
Who pulled her out?
Little Tommy Stout.
What a naughty boy was that,
To try to drown poor pussy cat,
Who never did him any harm,
And killed the mice in his father's barn.

There was a tailor had a mouse,
  Hi diddle unkum feedle!
They lived together in one house
  Hi diddle unkum feedle!

The tailor thought the mouse was ill;
  Hi diddle unkum feedle!
He gave him part of a blue pill,
  Hi diddle unkum feedle!

The tailor thought his mouse would die;
   Hi diddle unkum feedle!
He baked him in an apple pie.
   Hi diddle unkum feedle!

The pie was cut, the mouse ran out,
   Hi diddle unkum feedle!
The tailor followed him all about.
   Hi diddle unkum feedle!

The tailor found his mouse was dead,
   Hi diddle unkum feedle!
So he caught another in his stead
   Hi diddle unkum feedle!

Hie, hie, says Anthony,
Puss in the pantry,
Gnawing, gnawing,
    A mutton, mutton bone;
See how she tumbles it,
See how she mumbles it,
See how she tosses
    The mutton, mutton bone.

Pretty John Watts,
  We are in trouble with rats
Will you drive them out of the house?
  We have mice too, in plenty,
That feast in the pantry;
  But let them stay,
And nibble away:
  What harm is a little brown mouse?

The cat sat asleep by the side of the fire,
The mistress snored loud as a pig;

Jack took up his fiddle by Jenny's desire,
And struck up a bit of a jig.

Puss came dancing out of a barn
With a pair of bagpipes under her arm;
She could sing nothing but, Fiddle cum fee,
The mouse has married a bumble-bee
Pipe, cat—dance, mouse—
We'll have a wedding at our good house.

Hoddley, poddley, puddle and fogs,
Cats are to marry the poodle dogs;
Cats in blue jackets and dogs in red hats,
What will become of the mice and rats?